Tomi Ungerer

adelaide

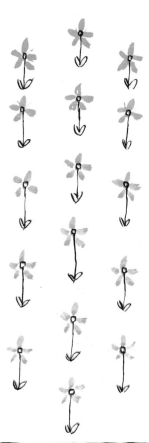

A DELL PICTURE YEARLING

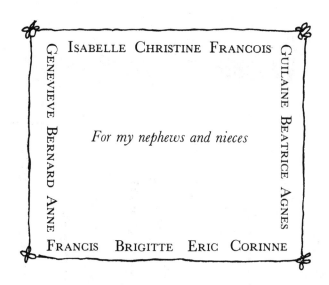

ISABELLE CHRISTINE FRANCOIS

GENEVIEVE BERNARD ANNE

GUILAINE BEATRICE AGNES

For my nephews and nieces

FRANCIS BRIGITTE ERIC CORINNE

Published by
Dell Publishing
a division of
Bantam Doubleday Dell Publishing Group, Inc.
666 Fifth Avenue
New York, New York 10103

The trademark Yearling® is registered in the
U.S. Patent and Trademark Office.
The trademark Dell® is registered in the
U.S. Patent and Trademark Office.
ISBN: 0-440-40571-8
Reprinted by arrangement with the author
Printed in the United States of America
November 1991

10 9 8 7 6 5 4 3 2 1

LBM

Adelaide's parents were surprised when they saw

that their daughter had wings.

As Adelaide grew, her wings became larger and larger.

She soon learned to fly.

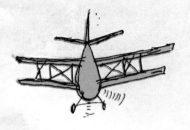

She liked to look at the birds and airplanes passing over the desert,

and wished she could travel too.

So one day she kissed her parents good-by and flew away.

Adelaide followed the first plane she met. The pilot was astonished.

When they finally landed, they were met by a cheering crowd.

Nobody had ever seen a flying kangaroo before.

The next day they flew on.

When Adelaide was tired she rested on the top of the plane.

They stopped at many places. In India they visited a rich maharajah.

When they reached Paris, Adelaide decided to stop traveling.

Sadly she said good-by to her dear friend, the pilot.

She was inspected by the customs officials.

Outside the airport Adelaide got into a cab. But she did not know she would have to pay for the trip. She had no money, and was embarrassed when the driver shouted at her.

However, a nice gentleman, Monsieur Marius,

was passing by. He paid her fare.

Monsieur Marius saw that Adelaide was tired and hungry.

So he invited her to dinner in a fine restaurant.

Then he took her on a trip through Paris.

From the top of the Eiffel Tower

he pointed out many interesting sights.

VICTOIRE DE
SAMOTHRACE

They visited

all the monuments and museums.

They saw many winged statues.

At Notre Dame. . . . .

Adelaide was frightened by the fierce gargoyles.

But the peaceful and lovely angels comforted her.

21

Monsieur Marius, who owned a theater, offered Adelaide a job in his show

She became a success overnight.

Her picture was on posters everywhere.

Adelaide led a happy life. But she often wished she knew another kangaroo.

Then one day when she was taking a walk she came upon a blazing fire.

A woman was crying and screaming.

Her two children were in the house.

Adelaide bravely flew through the smoke toward the children.

She put the baby in her pouch and the little girl on her back.

But the load was too heavy and she couldn't fly.

She fell all the way down.

Adelaide was hurt. But the two children were safe.

She was put in an ambulance.

When she awakened in the hospital, the grateful mother
and her children were there with flowers and candies.

Monsieur Marius brought Adelaide
magazines and newspapers. They
were full of stories about her bravery

After a time, Adelaide could walk again, with the help of a nurse.

She made little trips to a nearby zoo.

There she met another kangaroo called Leon.

They fell in love.

Adelaide went to see the zoo director.

She made him understand that she wished him to release Leon.

The director gave her a signed paper releasing Leon.

They were married soon after. Long live the happy couple!

Leon and Adelaide had many children. With her fine family

and good friends Adelaide was completely happy.